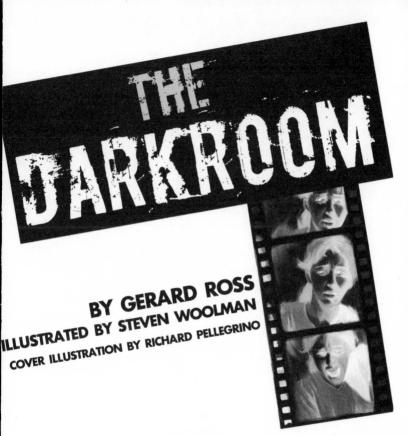

THE DARKROOM

BY GERARD ROSS
ILLUSTRATED BY STEVEN WOOLMAN
COVER ILLUSTRATION BY RICHARD PELLEGRINO

Librarian Reviewer
Marci Peschke
Librarian, Dallas Independent School District
MA Education Reading Specialist, Stephen F. Austin State University
Learning Resources Endorsement, Texas Women's University

Reading Consultant
Elizabeth Stedem
Educator/Consultant, Colorado Springs, CO
MA in Elementary Education, University of Denver, CO

STONE ARCH BOOKS

First published in the United States in 2008
by Stone Arch Books, A Capstone Imprint
151 Good Counsel Drive, P.O. Box 669
Mankato, Minnesota 56002
www.capstonepub.com

Text copyright © 1999 Gerard Ross
Illustrations copyright © 1999 Steven Woolman

First published in Australia in 1999 by Lothian Books
(now Hachette Livre Australia Pty Ltd)

Published in arrangement with Hachette Livre Australia.

Library of Congress Cataloging-in-Publication Data
Ross, Gerard.
     The Darkroom / by Gerard Ross; illustrated by Steve Woolman.
     p. cm. — (Shade Books)
     ISBN 978-1-4342-0792-0 (library binding)
     ISBN 978-1-4342-0888-0 (pbk.)
     [1. Grief—Fiction. 2. Photography—Fiction. 3. Cameras—
Fiction.] I. Woolman, Steven, 1969– ill. II. Title.
PZ7.R719654Dar 2009
[Fic]—dc22   2008008008

Summary: Emily finds out a mysterious secret about her dad's old
camera. It seems to be able to take picures of the future.

Art Director: Heather Kindseth
Graphic Designer: Kay Fraser

Printed in the United States of America in Stevens Point, Wisconsin.
032010
005721R

TABLE OF CONTENTS

Chapter 1

BACK TO THE DARKROOM

"Come on, Emily!" Tommy whined. "We need another player or we can't play soccer."

But Emily wouldn't move from her spot on the living room sofa. She used to enjoy playing with Tommy and his friends. She'd always been much bigger and faster than her brother, who was two years younger. But lately he'd started to catch up. His friends had, too. And they'd started to play rough.

Tommy might have caught up in size, but since she'd turned thirteen, Emily had become aware that the gap between them was bigger than ever.

That was clear when their father died. At the funeral, Tommy seemed to have become even younger. He held on to their mother like he was a little baby.

Emily had realized she needed to try as hard as she could to be strong. She had to help the family through its loss.

"Well, we don't want you to play anyway," Tommy said angrily. He stopped whining as soon as he figured out that he couldn't win.

He went outside. Emily just rolled over on the sofa. Maybe she should have played soccer. She didn't have anything else to do that afternoon.

She had looked forward to spring break all year. But now it was starting to be pretty boring.

She got up from the couch and began to walk around the house with her eyes closed. Her family always lived in the same house. She could make her way through every room with her eyes closed.

Emily stretched out one finger and gently slid it along the walls. She felt the smoothness of the paint in the hall. She felt the wallpaper in the dining room.

Her finger paused on the marks in the kitchen door's frame. The marks tracked Emily and Tommy's heights every six months.

Emily had first learned to walk around blind like this in the darkroom. Most of the time their dad used to work in there with the safe light on. The safe light was a dim red light that was safe for photographs.

Emily would feel her eyes get used to the dark. When he was loading film into the developing tank, her dad turned all the lights off. He even turned the safe light off.

Emily knew darkness better than any of her friends because of the time she'd spent in that room with her dad.

People think they know about darkness. They think night is dark.

Emily knew better. Even on a moonless night, with eyes closed tight, it still isn't really dark. You can still see shadows and movement.

But in the darkroom, without the safe light, you could open your eyes as far as they'd go. It wouldn't matter. Even if you stared as hard as you could, you would never see a thing.

Sometimes, though, it seemed like you could see something. Sometimes you thought there was something there. But that was just your imagination. That was just the darkness playing tricks.

Tommy never liked going into the darkroom. It scared him. He said it didn't, but that was a lie.

Emily remembered the time Tommy had freaked out in the darkroom. He yelled so much that their dad had opened the door before the film was safely in its tank.

A whole roll of film had been ruined. Emily had been furious with her brother, but their dad didn't get mad.

"I don't think there was anything special on that film anyway," he'd said.

That made Emily mad at her dad, too.

Today, Emily's fingers felt the marks in the door frame. The top marks were close together, since Tommy was catching up with her. Their dad used to carve the marks into the old wood with his pocket knife. They had stopped measuring eight months ago.

Emily opened her eyes and walked down the hall to their mom's office. Their mother worked from home now. When her husband died, she had left her job. She set up her own office at home.

Emily knew it was hard for her mom, especially during school breaks. So she tried to keep Tommy out of her mom's way as much as possible.

"Mom?" Emily asked quietly.

"Yes, honey?" her mother said.

"Is it okay if I get out Dad's camera?" Emily asked.

Her mother got up from her desk and went to Emily. She ruffled Emily's hair and hugged her.

"Of course it is," she said. "I was wondering when you were going to ask. You know your dad would want you to have his camera."

"I was thinking," Emily went on. "Maybe I could start the darkroom up again. I'll need some money for new chemicals, though."

"I suppose so," her mother said. "You make a list and I'll pick up what you need." Emily's mother smiled, but there was something strange in her voice. Something uncertain.

Chapter 2

DAD'S
CAMERA CASE

Emily sat with her legs crossed in the doorway of an open closet. Her father's camera case was between her knees. She slowly lifted the lid.

Before she opened the case far enough to see the camera, she smelled her father. Her memories of him had been growing fainter lately.

When she smelled that familiar smell, of vinegar and chemicals and plastic, the memories returned.

For a moment, she saw his easy smile, heard him laugh. She almost felt him hugging her.

She remembered standing next to him, looking at developing trays. They would watch the images appear like ghosts on the paper, soaking in the chemicals.

Her father seemed strange to people who didn't know him. Emily sometimes wondered how her mother had been able to see the man he really was. He was big and often clumsy. But he was a genius in the darkroom.

All her life, Emily loved to be in the darkroom with her dad. She would sit on one of the darkroom stools for hours.

Her dad would gently blow the tiniest dust spots from the negatives. His hands worked delicately under the enlarger lamp. He darkened a photo a little here, lightened it a little there.

The moment passed. Emily opened the camera case. There was an empty spot where her father's work camera used to be. Everything else was there.

Their dad had been a photographer for the police department. He took photos of crime scenes, fingerprints, broken glass. And dead people. Bodies.

That was what he did for a living. In his free time, he used his camera to make art.

He took photos of people he knew. He'd get Emily's mom to sit for hours under hot lights, wearing black in front of a white background.

He'd ask Tommy and Emily to sit close together and act natural. He didn't mind if that meant hair pulling, tickling, screaming, or tears.

The house was filled with his pictures, carefully framed and lovingly hung. Many more were stored in big folders in a closet or filed away in albums. They were getting dusty now.

Her father took photos of himself sometimes, when no one else would pose. He would dress in cool clothes. He'd mess up his hair. He'd pick a sheet to use as a backdrop.

Then he'd prop a mirror behind the camera. That would help him see what the scene would look like.

Emily loved those photos the most. She had one in a frame beside her bed. In it, her father looked scruffy and handsome. You could see in his eyes that he was a good man.

The photo by her bed was one of the last ones her father had ever taken. There was something special in it. Something sad in his face. Something that spoke to her.

It hurt when Emily realized that she couldn't remember what his voice sounded like.

Chapter 3

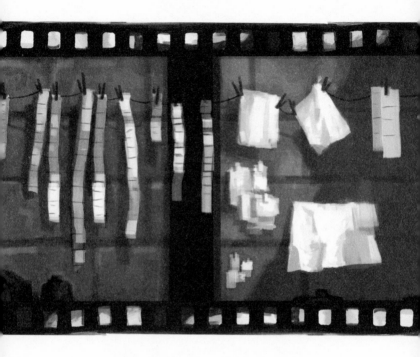

THE CAMERA

Emily looked inside the camera case. Her dad's fancy camera had belonged to the police department. When he died, they had taken it back.

That didn't bother Emily. She knew that the police camera wasn't the one he really used.

The fancy police camera was digital. It was big and expensive. It had cost more than two thousand dollars.

It had lots of buttons and dials and beepers. It made sure you got perfect pictures every time. All you had to do was press a button.

Emily's father had told her that he only carried the fancy police camera with him because his boss said he had to. He didn't really use it.

The camera he really used for everything was still in the case. It was a small, old, ugly camera.

Emily's dad's camera didn't do anything automatically. It wasn't even digital. It was the old-fashioned film kind of camera.

Her dad told her that it was the Rolls Royce of cameras. He said that all of the world's best photographers used the same camera. He said he would never switch to digital. He told Emily that he loved the darkroom too much. He knew it was really old-fashioned and it took longer, but he loved it anyway.

Emily's father had a book of photographs by a French photographer. All the photos in it had been taken with a camera just like his.

Emily looked through the book often. She loved all of the photographs inside.

There was a photo of a man sitting on a river bank eating bread and cheese. There was a photo of a man skipping across a puddle, almost touching his reflection. There was a photo of a little boy walking down a street with a big bottle. The boy looked just like Tommy. Even though she was often mad at her brother, it was Emily's favorite photograph.

Emily would never forget what her father had told her about why the best photographers used the same camera.

"Emily," he had said, "any camera can take a picture of someone's face. But this camera tells you things about that person. It can look into a person's soul. It tells you who they are. It tells you what they are. It tells you what will happen to them."

Those words made Emily's spine shiver when she remembered them. But she didn't realize their full meaning yet.

- Chapter 4 -

THE VOICE

"Leave me alone, Emily!" Tommy yelled. His sister was behind the couch, pointing the camera at him.

It was distracting, and Tommy was getting sick of it. He was trying to play a video game.

It was the tenth time that day that Emily had taken his picture. She took another one. Then Tommy threw a cushion at her, and she ducked.

"Mom!" he yelled.

Emily ran down the hallway into her room, laughing. She slammed the door behind her.

Emily had taken eleven photos of Tommy. She also had three shots of her mother, six of flowers in the garden, and four of Boof, the neighbor's black cat.

That made twenty-four. The roll of film was finished. Emily was finally ready to use the darkroom.

It was hot and bright that afternoon. But as Emily closed the darkroom door, the day disappeared. Inside the darkroom, it seemed like midnight.

Her mother had bought the things that Emily needed to get the darkroom going again. There were new bottles of all the chemicals she needed to develop the film and the pictures. There were also several sizes of the special photograph paper she would print the pictures on.

Emily had checked the equipment. She'd polished the enlarger lens, cleaned out the chemical trays, and dusted off the counter. She'd done everything just like her father had shown her.

"Dust is your enemy, Emily," he'd always said. She would never forget that.

To develop the film, Emily needed complete darkness. She checked with her hands to make sure she knew exactly where everything was.

Then she shut off all the lights. She pushed the button on the back of the camera. There was a click.

Then . . . was it a rush of wind? Was it a flash of some strange, greenish light from inside the camera? Or was it her imagination?

That's it, she thought. *Just my imagination.* The darkroom played tricks. Her dad had told her that.

Emily shook her head, as if to clear it. Then she went through all the steps her father had taught her.

She had already set everything up, so she was ready to start. She had only her hands to guide her. If she made a mistake, she would have to feel her way out of it. The tiniest drop of light would ruin everything.

Everything went smoothly. It was as if there was something — or someone — guiding her.

When the film was safely in the developing tank, Emily clicked the safe light back on again.

Emily carefully measured the developer into a large plastic container. She added water. Then she needed to check the temperature of the liquid. That would tell her how long to keep the film in.

It was a hot spring day. Outside, it was warm and sticky.

Emily put the thermometer into the liquid. She expected it to read about eighty degrees. The faint green glow of the dial said it was only sixty-eight degrees in the room.

Emily felt a sudden chill press against her back like cold fingers.

She kept the film in the tank for the right amount of time. She turned the tank every thirty seconds, just like her father had always done.

When it was ready, she poured out the liquid. There were more steps she had to follow, and more chemicals that she had to add to the film.

Finally, it was safe for Emily to turn the main light on again. She washed the film ten times in clean water.

Then she removed it from the tank and held it high above her head. The film curled slightly as it hung almost to the floor.

Emily looked at the twenty-four shots. Water dripped around her feet.

Most of the negatives looked good. It was hard to tell for sure at this stage, but it looked as if she'd gotten things right.

Then she thought she heard a deep voice, a calm and soothing tone. It said one word: "Good."

It must have been her imagination. It couldn't have been the voice she thought it was.

I must be dreaming, Emily told herself. *It must be the darkness, playing tricks on me. What I heard was just a door closing upstairs.*

"Emily!" a voice called. It was her mother. "Emily, honey, come on up. Dinner's ready."

Emily hung the negatives from a clip on the drying rack. Then she went upstairs.

Chapter 5

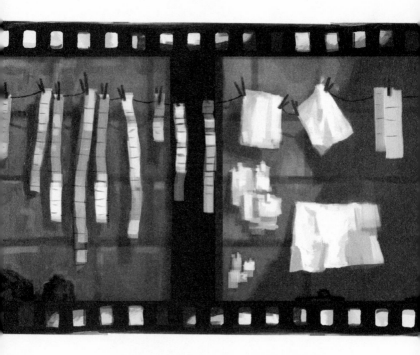

SUPERSTITION

"Hey, Squirt!" boomed a deep voice as Emily walked into the dining room. It was Uncle Pete, their mother's brother. He was sitting at the dinner table.

With one big hand, Uncle Pete was holding Tommy's arms down. He was stealing chips from Tommy's plate with the other.

"Didn't think you were going to join us," Uncle Pete said. "I thought I was going to have to eat your dinner for you, just like I'm doing for Tommy."

Tommy tried to say something. Uncle Pete stuffed some broccoli in his mouth to keep him quiet.

Tommy giggled and bits of green sprayed across the table.

"Peter!" Emily's mom said. She tried to look serious, but she couldn't help smiling.

Uncle Pete let go of Tommy and turned back to Emily. "So, Squirt," he said. "Your mom tells me you're using your dad's cameras. That's great."

Uncle Pete and Emily's dad had been on the police force together. That's how their dad had met their mom.

"Think you'll be taking photos for the force one day, like your old man?" Uncle Pete asked.

"Nope," Emily said. She shook her head. "I'm going to use my dad's camera to make art."

"Well, there is sort of an art to police photography," Uncle Pete said. He paused for a moment, his face serious. "Did you know that all the detectives always hoped your dad would be assigned to the cases they were on?" he asked Emily quietly. "They say the crimes were always easier to solve when he took the pictures. They say he could take photos of things that nobody else could ever see."

"Peter!" Emily's mom said. She looked serious too. "That's just superstition."

"Well, maybe, but if superstitions work, you use them. That's what cops think," Uncle Pete said.

He shot a nervous glance back at his sister. Then he changed the subject to dessert.

As soon as Emily had finished eating, she wanted to go back downstairs to check on her film.

Her mom noticed and said, "Don't worry, Emily. We'll clean up."

Emily rushed back downstairs and checked the film. She couldn't wait to print some of the photos she'd taken. But when she touched the ends of the hanging roll, it was still too damp to work with. There was nothing for her to do but wait.

When she was busy, the darkroom didn't bother her. But when she was just standing there waiting, everything seemed too quiet. She felt cut off from the world.

There was a big clock on the wall. As Emily waited for the film to dry, it reminded her of how long it was taking.

Emily went back upstairs. She told herself she was only leaving the darkroom because she was thirsty.

As she headed into the kitchen, she heard her mother and uncle at the dinner table in the dining room. They were talking in low voices. They hadn't heard her come upstairs.

"Don't be silly, Pete," Emily heard her mom whisper.

"All I'm saying is, maybe you should get her a different camera," Uncle Pete whispered back. "I mean, I think that it's great that Emily wants to take pictures, but why does she need to use that camera? You should get her something nice and new. And safer. A digital camera. Not that weird old one of her dad's."

"Peter, stop!" Emily's mom said. "You're being ridiculous. The whole thing is a stupid superstition." Her voice sounded shaky and upset.

Emily pressed herself against the wall and held her breath. *What's going on?* she wondered. *What's wrong with Dad's camera?*

"Is it ridiculous?" Pete asked. His voice was firmer. "Is it? You saw him the week before he died. He wasn't himself. He was scared. Nothing scared him before. He knew."

"I've had enough of this!" Emily's mom yelled. Her chair screeched as she stood up quickly. "It's late. I have to clean up."

Emily tiptoed out of the kitchen.

It wasn't late. What had made her mom so upset?

- Chapter 6 -

NEGATIVES

Emily pushed hard against the darkroom door. The door creaked loudly as she forced it open.

She knew the film would still need some more drying time. So, with the main light on, she opened the closet. It held several folders of old negatives.

Emily opened the first folder and flipped through the plastic pages. Everything looked strange in the negatives.

She'd never really thought about it before. She was so used to them. But now, as she tried to make out the images, she realized how ghostly, how unreal, people looked in negatives.

Everything was backward. Dark was light and light was dark. Trees seemed to be on fire. The sky always looked stormy. Smiles looked bigger, harsher, and stranger. They looked terrifying and gross, like the grins of skulls.

Between some of the pages were proof sheets. On each sheet, a couple of dozen stamp-sized photos brought the world back to normal again. The awful ghosts were changed back into people.

That made Emily feel better. But she still needed to find out what it was her father had known.

Emily thought about what Uncle Pete had said.

It was true. Her dad had acted very strangely in his last few days.

She remembered how serious he'd been. She remembered how closely he'd hugged Tommy and her. Tommy had squirmed and complained.

She remembered how much he'd hugged their mother that week. So gently. For so long.

Emily flicked through the pages, scanning the negatives, looking for answers.

There were nine folders in the closet. She had made her way through eight of them when the hairs on her neck stood up. Strange. Somehow, she knew that her film was ready.

Emily took the film down from the drying rack. She carried it over to the workbench.

Then she picked up the scissors to cut the roll into four strips. She counted out the first six negatives and carefully cut through the film. Then she cut the second. Then the third.

The fourth strip was too long. She counted the shots on it. Seven? She counted the other strips. Six on each. Twenty-five shots?

How could that be? She had only taken twenty-four pictures.

Emily held the strips up to the light. She tried to figure out what the extra photo was.

Finally, she realized what it was. It was Boof. There were five shots of the cat. But Emily was sure she had only taken four pictures of him.

In the extra shot, Boof lay on his side. His head was turned. He was lying on the road.

It didn't make sense. All of the photos Emily had taken of the cat had been near the bushes in the back yard.

There was something else that seemed odd. Something about the way Boof was lying. But Emily couldn't tell what it was from the negative.

She took the strip to the enlarger to make it big and print it. She worked quickly, her hands turning the knobs. Her heart pounded.

When it was all set up, she took out a sheet of photo paper. The tick of the clock seemed louder than before. The seconds lasted forever.

Emily tried to calm herself down by taking her mind, step by step, through the things she needed to do. Finally, the photo was ready to develop.

Emily took the paper to the developing tray. Carefully, she lowered the paper into the liquid. Ten seconds crawled by. Nothing. Fifteen. Nothing.

Then, all of a sudden, came the moment Emily had always loved most. It was the moment when the darkroom and the chemicals worked magic and a piece of blank paper turned into a photograph.

The picture of the cat slowly formed. Emily stared closely. She waited for hints to show up about where the photo had come from. The picture became clearer and clearer. Emily leaned closer.

The cat was definitely on the road. But that was impossible. Emily hadn't taken a photo out there. No one else had used the camera.

As the image darkened, Emily saw that there was something coming from Boof's nose and mouth. Something dark and thick.

Suddenly, someone pounded on the door, breaking the silence.

Emily spun toward the door. Before she could say anything, the room exploded into light. A small figure was standing in the doorway.

"Tommy!" Emily shrieked. "Get out!"

"Mom says you should go to bed now," Tommy yelled.

"How could you do that?" Emily screamed. "You never open a darkroom door like that!"

"I didn't know you had stuff out still," Tommy said. He remembered the rule their dad had taught them. "I'll close it now. I'm sorry."

"It's too late. You ruined my photo," Emily said. She turned back to the tray. The photo was already disappearing into a black blob.

Chapter 7

CLUES

Emily barely slept that night. She was furious about the ruined photo. And she was still puzzled by the strange facts that had been scattered in front of her that evening.

The next morning, Emily woke up when she heard voices outside. The only words she could hear were someone repeating, over and over, "I'm sorry."

Emily got out of bed and went downstairs. Her mother and Tommy were in the living room, looking out the front window.

"What's going on?" Emily asked.

Tommy turned. His face was a mixture of sadness and excitement. "Somebody hit Boof," he said. "Ran him over in a car. I think they killed him!"

"Come on, Tommy," their mother said. "Don't look, kids."

Emily didn't have to look. She already knew what she would see.

There wasn't time for the darkroom that morning. Tommy had a friend named Ben. Ben's family went up to the mountains every spring break. He'd invited Tommy on a camping trip.

So, right after breakfast, Emily and her mom helped Tommy carry his things out to the car. When they pulled up at Ben's place, Ben's family was standing around their big white SUV.

Their mother hugged Tommy close. She told him to be careful and to not tease snakes.

He turned to jump into the car. Then something made Emily grab her brother's shoulder to stop him.

She kissed him on the cheek and said, "Bye, Tommy."

"Yuck!" Tommy yelled, pulling away. Then he hopped into the SUV and slammed the door.

Ben's dad honked as they took off down the road. Emily's mom waved.

At home, Emily followed her mother into the office. The desk was in the middle of the room. It was right under a skylight that flooded the room with white light.

Everything felt warm, comfortable, and safe. But Emily knew she should be somewhere else. "I'm going downstairs for a while," she said, walking out of the room.

"Hey, I want to see some photos soon," her mother called after her.

It was cooler in the darkroom than it was upstairs. The air was still and thick.

Even though she didn't have any film or paper out yet, Emily turned the main light off. She wanted to work under the red safe light.

She returned to the folders of old negatives that she'd started looking through the night before. There must be a clue.

She looked at one page, then another and another. But she didn't even know what she was looking for.

As she lifted the last folder from the floor of the closet, something loose slipped out from its pages.

It was a negative strip, longer than all the others. With unsteady hands, Emily held the negatives up.

The first four looked like portraits of her father. She tried to figure out what the backdrop was. It looked like a beach.

Then she looked at the fifth shot.

Even though it was in negative, even though it was dark, even though the negative shook in her hands, she knew what she was looking at.

Emily slid to the floor, shaking her head. She closed her eyes, but she still saw the image in front of her.

Emily would always remember how it had looked.

The negative showed two hands sticking out of high ocean waves. One hand was small and thin. The other was strong and broad.

- Chapter 8 -

WAITING IN
THE DARKNESS

It had been awful weather for most of their vacation, eight months ago. But even when the sun finally broke through, they'd had trouble getting Dad to go down to the beach. Finally, he'd agreed.

As they'd walked down to the sand, they had seen a boy fishing. He was way out on the rocks.

Emily remembered how nervous her father had become. "What's he doing so far out there?" he shouted above the roar of the waves.

Then a huge wave broke across the rocks. It swept the boy into the sea. Someone had to help.

There was no one else around. Her father jumped in.

The boy and the man were caught in the current. Their bodies washed up two days later.

The two hands Emily remembered sticking out of the water were the hands in the negative.

But how could they be? Emily asked herself. *No one had a camera that day. And how could Dad have developed pictures of his own death?*

Uncle Pete had been right. Her dad had known he was going to die. The camera had seen it. The darkroom had told him.

It can't be, she thought. *It's the darkness. It's making me lose time, lose track, lose sense.*

"Emily," a voice said. It was deep, soothing. It came from all around her and held her like two caring arms.

"Daddy?" Emily whispered. She looked around. Nothing.

Then, out of the corner of her eye, Emily caught a small flash of green light. It was just like the one she'd seen when she opened the camera the day before.

The light had come from the enlarger. The negatives of Boof were still there.

Emily pulled the strip of negatives out and looked at them again. There was something different about the fifth photo.

She set it back in the enlarger and tore open her packet of paper. Quickly, she set one up and exposed it. Then she slid the paper into the developer.

The sound of the second hand seemed to boom out of the clock.

"Emily," the voice said again. "It's not your fault."

In the tray, an image was taking shape. It was an SUV. She'd seen it before.

This can't be happening, she thought.

A white SUV lay on its side at the edge of a steep, winding road. Horrified, Emily watched the image appear. The photograph showed a pair of legs hanging out of the SUV. The wreck was surrounded by clothes and cans of food and sleeping bags.

Tommy?

Emily spun quickly away from the tray. In a clumsy, shaking panic, her hands stumbled for the camera.

She wrapped her fingers around it and raised it above her head. She was ready to smash it down on the bench.

"No," the voice said, stopping her.

"Is it Tommy?" she pleaded. "Is he okay?"

"It's not always clear," the voice said. "You can't always tell. You must wait."

Emily put the camera down and looked around the room.

The voice spoke again. "Use this to see, Emily," it told her. "Look inside people. Learn from what their souls will show you."

"I'm not ready to see these things," Emily whispered. She was crying.

"It won't always be bad," the voice said softly. "You'll see beauty there too."

Emily wanted to say more. She wanted to hear more. But she felt something change in the air. It was as if the walls had been holding their breath and had just exhaled.

She knew the voice wouldn't speak again.

"Goodbye," Emily whispered. Her tears shone red under the safe light.

Outside, the future developed. Emily waited, alone in the darkroom, but she knew she couldn't wait forever.

ABOUT THE AUTHOR

Gerard Ross was born in Brisbane, Australia. He studied at the University of Queensland and Queensland University of Technology. His writing has appeared in various publications, and *The Darkroom* is his first story for children. He lives in Stockholm, Sweden, with his wife.

ABOUT THE ILLUSTRATOR

Steven Woolman was a designer and illustrator. He lived in Australia. He designed and illustrated numerous children's books, many of which won awards.

Steven passed away in 2004.

GLOSSARY

chemicals (KEM-uh-kuhlz)—substances that make other substances change or do things

darkroom (DARK-room)—a room with special tools for developing photographs

developer (di-VEL-uh-pur)—a chemical that causes an image to show up on a negative or photograph paper

enlarger (en-LARJ-ur)—a tool that makes images bigger

film (FILM)—a roll of thin plastic used in a camera to take pictures

lens (LENZ)—a piece of curved glass in a camera. Lenses bend light rays.

negative (NEG-uh-tiv)—a photographic film used to make prints

safe light (SAYF LITE)—in a darkroom, the red safe light will not harm a photograph

superstition (soo-pur-STI-shuhn)—a belief

thermometer (thur-MOM-uh-tur)—a tool used to measure temperature

DISCUSSION QUESTIONS

1. Whose voice do you think Emily hears at the end of this book?

2. Why is Emily's mother nervous about Emily using her dad's camera?

3. When Emily is bored, she decides to use her dad's camera. What are some other things she could have done? What do you do when you're bored?

WRITING PROMPTS

1. Emily's father was a photographer, and now Emily wants to be a photographer. What do your parents do? What do you want to do when you grow up? Would you want to have your parents' jobs?

2. Imagine that you have a camera that can take pictures of the future. One day, you discover one of the pictures. What does it look like? What does it show? What does it tell you about the future?

3. Emily used to enjoy playing with her brother, but she doesn't anymore. Do you have siblings? Do you like playing with them? Write about your siblings.

MORE SHADE BOOKS!
Take a deep breath and

CHRIS KREIE

THE CURSE OF RAVEN LAKE

BY CHRIS KREIE

▼▼ STONE ARCH *Fantasy*

Charlie has wanted to stay alone at his family's cabin for as long as he can remember. When he finally does, the day starts off perfectly. But then the old man next door mentions a curse. When darkness falls, something unseen scratches at the door . . .

Step into the shade!

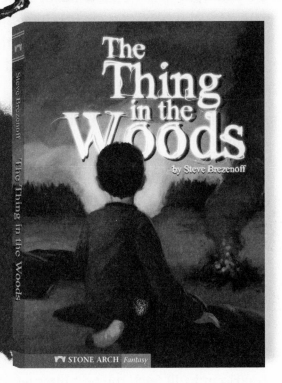

Jason and his dad have car trouble in the desert. They decide to camp overnight. Before they go to sleep, Jason's dad tells him a creepy story. When Jason wakes up, his dad is missing! It seems as though the ghost story is coming true!

INTERNET SITES

Do you want to know more about subjects related to this book? Or are you interested in learning about other topics? Then check out FactHound, a fun, easy way to find Internet sites.

Our investigative staff has already sniffed out great sites for you!

Here's how to use FactHound:

1. Visit *www.facthound.com*

2. Select your grade level.

3. To learn more about subjects related to this book, type in the book's ISBN number: **9781434207920**.

4. Click the **Fetch It** button.

FactHound will fetch the best Internet sites for you!